Barnyard Fable

G. Lowell Tollefson

Barnyard Fable

Contents

The Red Rooster

I'm a chicken. Nothing new about that. There are millions of us, probably billions. We turn up everywhere: crowing on a fence, strutting in a field, pecking for seeds, insects and stones along a roadway, getting flattened there sometimes, or even ending up between hamburger buns. They always say the same thing about us. Why does a chicken cross the road? To get to the other side, stupid! By stupid, they really mean us.

Well, that's the point. I'm not stupid. I guess I'm a freak of nature, since I was born with a mind. A chicken with a mind. Imagine that. God has a sense of humor. My head is a little larger than those of most chickens, and I've had problems with it too, gotten into a few nasty fights. Especially with some of the older hens when I was little. There's something about provincial women. Narrow. But the problem gave me a unique perspective on the whole. I realized how misunderstood we are. I mean chickens, all of us. We're a unique part of nature too, and I'd like to tell you about it. So I'll begin at the beginning.

First, I was born out of an egg, not a warm, comfortable womb. It makes a difference, kind of hardens your perspective on life right at the start. You can't begin to imagine how cramped life is inside of an egg. An egg is a hard-walled uterus. It's like being encased in cement. You've got your feet jammed up in front of your face like a conductor in a train wreck, and there's nothing you can do about it. A certain amount of light, air, and moisture can pass through the shell, but you can't imagine the joy that comes after the breakout! You hammer away from the inside with your egg tooth, and you've got temporary muscles in your neck that would intimidate an ox. Eventually the shell falls away in pieces and you push yourself out. Then you just lay there limp and wet as a jellyfish. Getting out of that cell is hard work.

So you just lay around and dry off. That's what I did. I don't remember every detail. How much do you remember of your birth? Mom had hollowed out a nest in the sand on the floor of the chicken house, instead of in one of the boxes, and there were some downy feathers in it. But sand is made out of miniature rocks, and it was a relief when my feathers dried and the hard grit stopped sticking to my body. I stood up. Some of my brothers and sisters were already active and others were still coming out of the egg. There was one egg that was dark under the shell and cold if you fell against it. Disgusting. I don't know why Mom hadn't pushed it out of the nest. Didn't smell bad though.

It wasn't long before we left the henhouse and went out into the yard. Cool green grass, fresh air, sun, a pleasant little breeze. You cannot imagine it. It was heaven already, especially after that dark henhouse and the gritty nest. There were grasshoppers all around too, and my brother Henry caught one. Yes, I named my brothers and sisters. I was sort of the Adam of the barnyard, going around naming everything, you know, but it meant nothing to the rest of them. Anyway, this one little brown grasshopper that Henry got caused pandemonium. Everyone was trying to grab and run off with it at once. It got so crazy, several of us ran off with it in different directions at the same time.

Every morning Mom took us out before dawn. We'd be out there peeping in the soft predawn air with only the slightest hint of the coming light, and Mom would cluck softly now and then in the stillness to keep us near. It was cold at that hour and we'd gather in the warm places under her feathers for relief, crowding in, climbing over one another, trying to get where it was warmest, sticking our heads out from under her wings. Then we could see the whole world out there and be comfortable at the same time. Moms are useful that way.

Eventually the sun would come up over the trees and lay its warm belly on everything. That felt really good! Didn't need Mom anymore, and she'd have to cluck like a steam locomotive to keep us in line.

Well, that's how it all started. But, if I go on like this, it'll take days to tell the story. So I'll just pick an incident or two to give you a feel for what it's like to be a chicken.

I must've been getting up there in the months. It was the middle of summer. I had all my feathers, not to mention the beginnings of a flashy new tail, and I was getting my comb and spurs. I was starting to notice some of the young pullets too. Figured I'd gather a few to myself, seeing as there were plenty to go around. You can tell I was feeling my corn scratch. The blood runs hot in that first summer when you start to get your spurs! I was a fine looking fellow, big for my age, red on my back with gold spangles on my neck and that iridescent green black tail in the making. The envy of the barnyard, I figured. More than one hen would scuttle down on her belly for me. I'd seen the young pullets show themselves nervous in my presence, and I didn't like the way the old roosters were eyeing them either. There were two of those guys, so I figured it was time to stake my claim before they moved in on what, by rights, ought to be mine. After all, they had plenty of the big ladies already, more than enough for a couple of old codgers on their last legs.

So I got up on a stump. Nobody had told me what its principal use was. And I belted out my song. Well, I'm embarrassed to admit it came gurgling up my neck like water in a clogged pipe. It sounded like a zither, a Jew's harp, and an out of tune trumpet thrown in together. I was absolutely mortified, and the two big boys took note of it too. So I hopped down and hid myself in some bushes for awhile. I needed a dust bath anyway. My feathers were getting a little oily.

Anyway, when I came out from that dust bath, one of the big fellows was waiting for me. Just sort of pecking around in the grass and turning his head and big golden eye in my direction now and then. When I appeared, giving my feathers a last shake and a little preening action, he stretched out his neck and flapped his wings. He was a big gray ox of a fellow, with massive golden legs like pillars on a courthouse and spurs the size and gleaming sharpness of a scimitar. I could feel my heart take a plunge and a couple of leaps in different directions, like it wanted to leave me on my own to handle the mess but couldn't find a way out.

The big fellow ambled on over kind of sideways, pecking now and then, like he was looking for something in the grass and didn't see it, and like he had plenty of time to take care of small matters. Well, he saw me well enough. I wasn't standing up tall or anything. In fact, I wouldn't have minded melting into the ground. So when he got right up to me, he just turned around in my direction and puffed out his neck feathers. Gad! There was nothing I could do but put out a feather or two myself. To tell the truth, I was feeling a little sick and none too steady on my feet. But I resolved to give it my best, sick-hearted though I was.

It didn't last long. We circled a bit, sizing each other up. He was trying to decide on the best approach for committing murder, and I was trying to see if there was any end to him, or if the sun was just in eclipse. There's no sense getting into the details. He hit me a couple times like a medicine ball and I was through for the day. I limped back into the bushes and lay there panting, my beak wide open and dripping. He did a little crowing from the stump I had used and then went on about the business of eating to make himself bigger—if that was possible—and, of course, devouring hens. I didn't even have enough spirit left to feel jealous.

But on every clouded horizon there is a sun-dappled new beginning. It was kind of a shocker at the time, but the results were in my favor. It was several months later and I'd gotten to be a pretty good-sized fellow myself: red as fire, golden as the sun, and flashing a magnificent tail that curved over my back end big as a rainbow. Some of the more mature hens were beginning to take notice. I began to sense that a number of them were doing their feeding in whatever quarter I had chosen to hunt in for the day. One of the big roosters was gone. I'm not sure what happened to him. But Big Gray was still there, and I wasn't sure I wanted to take him on again. He'd done some serious damage to my self-esteem, and I figured just a few scrawny female castoffs would be good enough for me. He could have all the better egg-laying machines. I don't mean any disrespect to the hens. They were all looking good. It's just that I wasn't feeling brave enough to be particular.

Well, Old Gray was a selfish, conceited fellow who couldn't settle on losing anything. He had to have them all. So I was running on dry, as you can imagine. Then a miracle happened. God works in strange ways. One day the Great Feeder—that's what I call him—he walks on two legs like us but is featherless, naked and ugly as sin. One day the Great Feeder comes out into the barnyard and corners Old Gray. He grabs him up, then takes him over to our singing stump. You know, the one where I lost my youthful cockiness.

There's an ax by the stump, leaning against it. I know what an ax is now, but I didn't then. He lays Old Gray on his back, kind of bewilderedlike with his neck stretched out and looking a little wild in the eyes. Like I must've looked the day we fought, I can't help thinking. He lays him out, picks up that ax, and whack! There are two Old Grays. The bigger part, bleeding like a fountain and flopping around without any direction. The smaller part just laying there looking up at the sky with one eye until it glazed over.

My troubles were over. It was like waking up to a great inheritance or suddenly discovering you had become a baron. It was all mine. I had become the master of innumerable hens, and it had happened without my lifting a spur. Isn't God good!

The Pullet

Botheration! Everywhere I go these roosters are all over me. What's a hen to do—sit on eggs day and night? What kind of life is that? Henpecked! Did I hear "henpecked?" Ha ha ha. Or maybe it's cluck cluck cluck. How does a chicken laugh anyway?

My point is, you've got this barnyard with a stump in the middle of it and an ax propped against the stump. The stump is the middle of our world. Everybody knows about it. We revolve around it like meaty little planets, and it's the door we go out of when we leave this world. The god takes care of that. I don't really like him. I'm afraid of him, but that's the way he made us—two-legged like himself.

I can't seem to get to my point. It's this: I want to live! I mean really live. We've all gotta go sometime. We shouldn't act like dead meat before we do. Yes, I'm henpecked by roosters. I don't do the henpecking, even though I'm a hen. They do it. All those randy young roosters we've got. Boy, we've got a lot of them this year. And that red one is one of the worst. He wants every egg on the place to have his stamp on it. It's kind of his logo: here I am, the mighty red randy rooster, or something.

Well, it's true, I'm just barely a hen. I'm a pullet. I'm the same generation as all these young roosters. It's just that the numbers didn't come out right. Too few of us pullets, and the old hens are two big, picky, and feisty. I saw red boy there try to mount one the other day. It was better than a rodeo, not that I've ever seen one.

I'm not ready for motherhood anyway. Laying an egg is like swallowing a big rock and then trying to pass it. Miserable business. I don't recommend it. But I am getting more used to it. They're coming about one every other day now. Like hornets in a closed room. They've gotta be dealt with. This morning I got up on a fence and laid one. Smack. Everyone came running to eat the yolk. The god was angry too. He said I was the most useless young hen he ever saw. I don't understand the gods—there's more than one of them. But a very old hen friend of mine told me that's what he said and I'd better watch out. She was talking about the stump with the ax.

This old hen might be the grandmother to the red rooster. She's red like him but not as pretty. That's right, pretty. Just ask him. Look at him over there now, strutting around like he owned everybody. That's why I'm hiding in these bushes. I also want to get some advice from my friend. She's cooling herself off and taking a sand bath under these bushes.

"Hello," I says. I'm speaking now about the past because it's been awhile since I talked to her. Randy Red is laid up under a nearby bush because the midday sun is mighty hot.

"Why, hello," she says to me in a low cluck. "Where have you been?"

"Avoiding randy Red and his crowd."

"Well, I wouldn't worry about them. The god will thin them out, and only the strongest will survive."

"I know, but I can't outrun the strongest of them. Why doesn't he thin them out instead?"

"Don't know. Just seems to turn out that way. Whatever is pleasantest is always just around the corner and never seems to come into plain sight. You've gotta roll with the punches, young lady. That's how you get to be an old bird like me. Stay low and let all the flack pass over your head. That means no squatting on fences to lay an egg. The god wants them whole. Don't know what he does with them, but you'd better get with the program, or he'll be thinning you out too."

"I know, I know. I'm working on it. But I wanted to get some advice, if you don't mind."

"Oh sure. I don't mind. What's an old clucker for anyway?"

"Well, what I want to know is, how do you get into the grain bin? When the god tosses the seed out on the ground, I always come up short. I'm not strong and bold like some of the others, and I always get shut out, like they were a door and I was a fly."

"Sure, I can understand. I used to be a young pretty thing like you. It's not all hunger either. It's jealousy. So I'll tell you what to do, but you'd better be careful. You're not on good terms with the god now. Whew! You don't want to come up head short, let me tell you."

Well, I'm at the grain bin now. It's not going to be as easy as I thought. The grain bin is inside a shed attached to one side of the henhouse. The shed's open on one side, and the bin is at the back, the bottom of it a little off the ground to keep the grain dry. There are some barrels in the shed too, closed up tight. The god takes things from them, like cracked corn, mash, and a little seed and mixes them together to put in the bin.

What the old red hen told me is that the god usually puts the lid on loosely, leaving it a little ajar. And from the looks of things, that's true. All I've got to do is fly up there, walk out onto the loose end, and the whole thing will come off. Of course, I'll come off with it, but, if I'm careful, I won't get hurt. Then I can just fly back up there and kerplop, I'll be standing in the middle of grain heaven.

But, as I said, there's a problem. A duck, for Pete's sake! They don't eat the same mix we do. His bin is over there, closed up tight. So there he is, walking back and forth, too dumb to figure out how to get the top off. He can't just reach down from the edge where the lid's ajar because the grain level is too far down. And if he hopped down with the lid still on, he'd probably never get out.

So what am I to do? Though some of the other chickens talk to the ducks, I can't get the hang of their harsh, guttural voices. It grates in my ears. I've gotta work on this. Cogitate a little. It's a cinch we're not going to have a neighborly chat. Ducks aren't conversational, and I wouldn't understand him anyway.

Wait. I've got it. I'll fly up there and try to coax him out onto the overhanging end of the lid. With two of us on it, there's no doubt it's going to fly. Then we can both get back up there and eat to our heart's content.

But he's so big and fat. What if he gets out on the end before I do? Down he goes and I get slung into the wall. No, that's no good. Wait a minute. Wait. Wait. He's too dumb to figure it out that easily. If he wasn't, he would've already done so. All I've got to do is be quick and nimble. If anything goes wrong, I go into orbit before the lid moves. Then I'm safe and the lid's off. Okay, here I go.

Wow! He sure looked startled. Me coming up here like a bat in the semi-dark. Shut up, will you! You're going to have the whole neighborhood in here.

Oh no. Not that way. We don't want to go out onto the edge before I get there. Stop making so much noise, will you. Oh, here comes the god. I've gotta get out of here.

You're never going to believe this. That big fellow got out onto the edge of the lid before I could think, and it was like putting a horse on a two wheeled wooden wagon. Everything went flying before I could think, the god shouting, and Mr. Duck heading for open spaces.

Now I'm at the bottom of this thing, and the lid came down right back on top, tighter than before. There's no way I can fly up and get out of that tiny opening. I'm stuck. Stuck till the god finds me and takes me over to the stump. You didn't warn me of this, mamma red. Lordy, lordy, whatever am I going to do. Dumb duck. Why do there have to be ducks in this world.

Well, I've got plenty of food. But no water. Oh lordy, no water in this hot weather and me shut up in this place. I think my feathers are going to fall off.

What's that? The god? No. I've been here for hours, days maybe. I don't know. I went through one long dark spell. I guess that's a day. Always has been before. That means it's morning, and the god's gonna come and get feed. I'd better start practicing on how to lie on a stump. Peaceable like. I don't want an undignified end, wings akimbo, toes curled, eyes wide, beak gaping. Disgusting.

Oh. I hear something. Be still chicken heart. This is the end. This is how you go to heaven. I don't want to go to heaven. I want to stay here. Well, not down here, but in the world. Oh, what's the use? Now I lay me down to sleep . . . .

Who's that? I heard someone fly up here. The gods don't fly. Their wings are too skinny. Well, I'll be. Never thought I'd be glad to see him.

That's how it was. The red rooster got me out. Can you imagine that? Of all people. Chickens, I mean. I had to explain to him how to do it, how the old red hen told me, but he did it and I'm free. I owe my life to that randy bugger. Well, there are worse things than that.

The Duck

I'm a duck, a puddle duck. All ducks are puddle ducks. At least that's what they say. I'm shaped like a boat, and I walk with my belly level to the ground, just in case there's a flood. Some of the chickens think I'm dumb, like that young pullet over there. She almost put me under the guillotine with her own foolishness.

Chickens think poorly of ducks like me because we walk around so awkwardly on land. I'll bet they'd think someone from outer space was funny too, just before they all got sucked into his spaceship for chicken stew. But I'm not a vindictive fellow. I'm pretty laid back. Let them cackle and laugh. Bunch of old hens.

Here's the main story, duck gabbling aside. It's about how we handle things. I and my kind are a lot better with dogs than they are. Let a dog give a woof, and they all shoot straight up into the air. Now I ask you, with short distance flyers like chickens, where are they gonna go? Why straight on back down for lunch, I reckon. Now that's a mighty happy dog.

Now the master . . . . We ducks aren't into deities. Some of my cousins travel thousands of miles twice each year, and they know who tied down the ends of the world. It was the great archduck, but we won't get into that, since none of us have ever seen him.

As I was saying, the master has a child. Don't know how anything like that could've ever fit into an egg, but it must've happened once. Ha ha ha. Quack quack quack. I can just see it. Stand up, young fellow! And he hits his head on the shell of the egg. "Help, I'm trapped." He can't get out because, in spite of all of those pearly white teeth, he's got no egg tooth. There he sits, rolled up like a bent worm in a shell. They do look like worms. Slippery too, when you get the fake feathers off them.

Anyway, this little master—this little two-legged, halfwit, ax-wielding pariah of the barnyard—it's not enough that we've got him. He's got a dog too. You know what a dog is: a slavering, loll-tongued, brainless battering of barks. If the dog doesn't get you, the ax will. That's why there's a boy. He's gotta prove something. I mean, he's *born* having to prove something. That's why there's an ax. I don't know. Goes together something like that. Trying to untangle these mysteries gives me a headache.

The dog's the main point. We'll save the little master for later. Put him back in the egg, so to speak, till we need him. The dog comes around the house, lolling his big tongue in the midday heat, his eyes big and mournful, like he wishes there weren't so many feathers on all the meat. He comes around and, wham, straight away all the chickens are hung in the air like stars in the firmament.

Of course, they can't stay up there, so down they come and hit the ground running, squawking, fluttering their wings, gad! what a sight! The dog, he doesn't know which way to go, turning his head every direction and barking ferociously. It's like he's giving directions to an orchestra but can't remember what he did with his baton.

The musicians, they're every one playing his own tune. The dog gets to the stump and does a wheelie. I mean, he rears up on his hind legs, tongue lolling, and says, "Come on, fellas, this ain't the way you make music." He gets up on the stump and looks around.

Some of the chickens are on top of the chicken house, but they don't stay there. They're too scared to know they're safe and jump back down. Now the dog's off the stump.... Well, you know the rest of the story. He catches one. And all the while I'm standing in the middle of the barnyard without ruffling a feather. Dog never noticed me. And I'm pretty wide in the hips too.

No, I'm not a woman. We're all like that. It's not just for egg laying. It's for boating too. Of course, there isn't much water in the barnyard. But there's water in the horse trough in the adjacent field. We keep our seamanship intact over there. Horses don't like it, but that's alright.

Well, this is the part that's difficult to tell. I take a lot of ribbing from some of those chickens. Not the old hens with their wide aprons of feathers. Not the old roosters with their palm tree tails. They're in a world of coupling, competing for the ladies, laying eggs, and raising chicks that leaves no time for any other sport. But the young ones, those pullets and cockerels, aren't they a sight? They think they're all grown up, and they aren't. Ducklings are much better behaved. It's the decorum of the water-borne world. You gotta know how to line up.

What's so difficult to tell about this is my involvement. You see, I may not always get along with some of the chickens, but we're all in it together when it comes to the dog.

So I says, "Quack quack." That's to let him know I'm coming. Give him a warning. I don't travel very fast on my feet, but I've got my head low to the ground and my neck stretched out. In more ways than one if this doesn't work out.

I don't actually fly, but I use my wings to lift my feet off the ground. And into the fray I go. What a mess of feathers there were already. With that dog there's no fooling around. I hit him a good one on the ear. I hear him yelp, and I'm out of there. Believe me, I'm out of there!

But that moment was long enough for him to let go of the chicken, and she scuttled out of there faster than a weasel in a henhouse, feathers flying. No, not from the weasel. From the chicken. Disgusting. I don't want to think about weasels. I just needed the image.

That dog was as bewildered as I think I've ever seen him. Kind of like someone coming up and smacking you on the head while you've got a mouth full of peanut butter sandwich. I don't know where I got that one. Picked it up somewhere.

The dog stands there looking bewildered. He was probably asking himself, "Has that chicken got two heads? What hit me?" Ha ha ha. Quack quack quack. Thank the archduck he didn't know it was me. I'm just standing a little off to the side like a passenger on a platform when the express train goes by. Minding my own business and counting heads on the train.

The dog backs up a little and tries to spit some of the feathers out of his mouth. They're stuck like flypaper to his tongue and lips. It wasn't even the shadow of a meal. The chickens are all calm as unraked leaves now. One or two of them are looking sideways at the scene, clucking softly. But most want to just blend in with the ground and whatever bush happens to be available. The one who got away is a bit denuded, but that's just an embarrassment. New feathers will grow in.

Oh, by the way, there are other ducks on the farm. I just happened to be most available to save the day. We do that.

Over there in dog town our one participant has lost all interest in chicken bouillon. If that's the soup du jour, he'll leave it for another day. He turns and goes off back around the house, tail a little less elevated than before.

Years ago—I'm not as young as I look—there was an old philosopher duck, bearded with all that red stuff around the face. He said a dog only attacks once on any one day because the distance between his ears is too short for any complex electric circuitry. That old philosopher isn't with us anymore. He neglected to figure on the little master with the ax and any resentment he might have about his dog. You see, we're all kind of heroic like that. Comes from our cousins and ancestors flying so far through great storms.

After my own personal encounter with the dog, my status in the barnyard grew quite a bit. More than one chicken noticed that not a single rooster had joined the fray. Imagine all that proud strutting and flashing of spurs and bright colored ensigns. Means nothing, it appears.

A number of chickens young and old gathered around me after the dog left. It seems they wanted to know how I mustered the courage to do it and why. I couldn't really say, other than that it sort of came natural. They just stood around me gawking, turning their heads and clucking softly. Wouldn't let up their looking, like they'd never see a duck before. I have to admit I hammed it. It's not every day you can feel as important as the archduck.

The Wedding

Chicken weddings aren't elaborate affairs. Maybe that's because the whole arrangement is kind of loose, with a random coupling here and there. A little spice in the barnyard, they call it. It keeps things interesting and sets up an electric current among the hens. They never know what's coming.

Nevertheless, there is such a thing as a chicken wedding. It happened when I took my first pullet, a sweet thing but kind of naive. She almost got herself buried in the grain bin. I took a shine to her because I liked her tail. Now, let's not get vulgar. If you want to put it that way, I like them all. And I let them know it too. That's what I mean by an electric current.

No, this one is different. I'm into sweetness like a bee into honey, and she had this cute little golden tail. That's what drew me to her, kind of sidling up, you know. Besides, she was the first one, and you don't take on the big cluckers for that. You save them for later, like a hearty stew, and eat your desert first. At least I do.

Anyway, with Old Gray down and into the land of God, or nod, whichever it was, I moved in to claim the barnyard as my own. I said to myself, counting as I went, "I could have this one or that one or how about this one over here?" But counting is one thing. The old ladies warm up to a young fella kind of slowly. They've gotta get over the mother complex.

So, as I say, I took a shine to little Golden Tail there and thought that was as good a place as any to start my matrimonial adventures. She knew about as much about it as I did, and so I figured I could get the drop on her. But two virgins don't make an egg, as they say.

Truth told, I wanted the big mammas to have a look at my prowess. Then they'd welcome me with open wings. Oh, those warm breasts! But it was more than that. I'm a bit of a romantic. I really did take a special shine to little Golden Tail. That's why I decided to go whole rooster and make it a wedding.

A wedding is different from the general kind of barnyard cavorting. You do the barnyard routine because it's a duty. The great provider needs the eggs. He gets the eggs, we get grain. It's as simple as that. No ceremony required, once you're warmed to it. But getting the old hens warmed is the thing.

Yes, yes, I know. Eggs don't have to be fertilized. But do you think I'm going to shout that out in the barnyard? You must be out of your mind. What the masses don't know is best left that way. That's just good leadership.

So here's the plan. There's a bucket out in the yard. A pail turned upside down. Sweet little Golden Tail likes to eat down there, pecking around the edges of the bucket. I don't know what draws her to it. Maybe there are some bugs trying to stay in the shade. Beetles have got those shiny dark carapaces that take in too much sun. Maybe that's it.

Anyway, I figured I'd just sidle on over and start up a little conversation. You know, "How are the beetle éclairs today? Have they got soft centers?" It always warms a woman's heart when you compliment her finesse in choice of food. Especially a young one who isn't sure of her culinary skills. I figured I'd say a few sweet nothings like that, then get up on the bucket. Keep the smooth talk flowing, almost like the soft clucking of a mother hen. It gets them every time.

How do I know that, being a virgin? Well, it's instinct, I guess. Some of us robust types come equipped with a sharp eye for these things. For instance, I knew I was destined to be cock of the rock in the barnyard. It was just a matter of defeating Old Gray.

But the wedding's the thing. What makes the first time a wedding? Well, nothing really. But you never forget it. It's more ceremonious somehow. That's what makes it a wedding. My mother told me that, though she wouldn't tell me who my father was. I don't think it was Old Gray. I don't think it mattered to her who it was anyway. It was more like a general impression.

"He got the drop on me," she said, "like thunder out of the clouds. I was just a mess of feathers." But she didn't seem to care about it other than that. Just the thunderclap and all.

I admit, it's hard to explain a wedding. You get up a lot of fuss and bother to do one. There's ceremony, you know, and proper decorum. The whole barnyard comes to see a wedding. But after that, it business as usual.

At any rate, what I was originally going to say is that, once up on the bucket, I figured I could get the drop of my darling. She'd be so pleased, knowing how I tricked her. It shows cunning and forethought, the kind of guy you want to have around to change the light bulbs.

So off I go, right over to the bucket. And there she is in all her glory, a beetle in her beak. She could've had a rose between her teeth and a golden curl of feather around her ear and she wouldn't have looked any more enchanting. I could feel myself shudder with anticipation.

I said, "How are you doing, Golden Tail?"

She said, "Mmm, mmph, gulp." She was still working on the beetle. Afterwards, she wiped her beak on the grass, once each way. She had all the delicate manners of a lady. Just knowing how delicate and refined she was set me on fire. There was something in her manners. Made me hotter than a sun-baked lizard. I had about as much stored up energy too.

"That was a sour one," she said, squinting one eye. "Must've been a young one."

"Yeah, it probably was," I added wisely. "Beetling season has only been on a short time. They haven't had time to ripen."

"I prefer grasshoppers," she said.

"Those long slender bodies without the carapace. I can't say as I blame you."

She opened her beak in a smile. A little water dripped out. It was a hot day. I knew I had her on a string.

So I got up on the bucket. Wow! This is my first time, I thought. And to think it's about to happen. I was shaking so much the bucket started wobbling.

Golden Tail cocked one eye up at me like, "Has he got all his marbles?"

But I wasn't deterred. Conquest is sweeter than honey. But, what would bees know? Most of them are sterile. I said, "It's a beautiful day." Like every lover, I was oozing with poetry.

"If you say so," she clucked matter-of-factly. She had returned to her business of searching around the edges of the bucket. "Found another beetle," she squawked, lifting it with delight.

The time was at hand, and I pounced. Off the bucket I came, like potatoes pouring into a root cellar. I was all over the place, and by the time I hit the ground, she was gone. She didn't go far. She just stood at a little distance, looking at me like, What was that?

I picked myself up off the ground, feeling embarrassed. So embarrassed, in fact, I decided to preen my wings.

"What a conceited fellow!" she clucked and wandered off pecking the ground here and there.

There was a considerable row over at the henhouse, all the old matrons cackling up a storm. They'd seen the entire incident and had noted my failure. "Well, the eggs will have clear yolks this year," one of them said with laughter. They all thought that a good one, and the cackling went up in an even bigger roar and probably lifted the clouds.

I was so ashamed of my unmanly performance, I almost wished I was a capon. I slunk off to some bushes to nurse my wounded pride. Chickens have pride, you know. Have you ever seen a rooster lose a fight? Some of them won't eat for days, or maybe never. It's a miserable business being without your manly self-respect. Especially when there are so many witnesses and all of them eligible egg-layers.

I laid around for awhile in the cool dust, but it was a hot afternoon, and I was charged up like a loaded rifle. My firing pin was humming with tension. I needed to get a round off that day. So up I sprang again and was off at a run. I was thinking, I don't care about decorum.

She was over by the bucket again, and I plowed into her like a witness to a fire. Didn't matter if I was on fire or had seen one. It was all the same in an emergency like this. I flipped her clear over, but she was back on her feet before I could think. She was back on her feet and off across the yard to the henhouse. She disappeared into its cool depths.

I rested on the ground panting. This is not going well, I concluded. Why does such a simple thing have to be so difficult? Why, only a little while ago I saw two dragonflies going by tied in a knot. Couldn't tell which was the engine and which the caboose. All of nature is coupling like the two ends of a rainbow, and I'm sitting in the middle with no pot of gold.

But I got up in the midst of an incredible cacophony of cackles. Every hen on the place was amused by my failures and had left off feeding to discuss the comical events. The young cockerels were amused too. Modestly, of course. I was the biggest of the bunch. But that might not always be the case, and I needed to stake my territory while I could. A miner that's not sitting on his claim doesn't gather much gold.

It was about then I noticed the young lady peering demurely out the door of the henhouse. I thought, What could she be up to? A shaft of golden sunlight fell along her lovely neck and back, and I swear, they never made a kimono that looked better on a woman. If she'd have had a fan, I'd have been a fly.

I gave myself a good shake to get the dust out of my feathers, and that gave the old cacklers a row of laughter. But I didn't care. My heart was a milkshake churning in a blender. My insides were all chilly, fluid, and lumps whirling about in confusion. I didn't know what my fate would be, but I was heading over to that henhouse.

Just then the dog came around the big house. He'd had a rough time of it a few days before, but he thought he'd put in another lick. The old cacklers were suddenly stone silent, and, since I was out in the middle of the yard, he headed for me.

I did something I never thought I would do. I turned and faced him. What else could I do with so many witnesses? He pulled himself up short not more than a yard from me and let loose with his barking. His hackles were up on his neck, and so were mine, but his tail was wagging. His shoulders were down, and he looked like he half wanted to play. I don't think he knew what he wanted.

But I did. I'd had it for one day. All the shame and embarrassment had cost me my self-respect, and I was ready to put some kind of a down payment on redemption. I could see my intended over there looking a little startled. I flew at the dog and struck out with my spurs. He yelped and headed back around the big house.

I think I mentioned once before that I had a big head. Well, it got a lot bigger. I had just defeated the dog. Amazing! There was silence all around. No one could believe it anymore than I could. Could this be me? I put one foot on the other to see that it was mine.

Then I struck out over the yard and went right up to that young pullet. I said, "What you got cooking, baby?" No, I didn't say that, but I wanted to. Truth is, I couldn't think of anything at all to say. We just stood there and eyed each other.

She stepped back into the door of the henhouse, and I followed her in. Now I suppose you're wanting some kind of voyeuristic description. Well, it's not going to happen that way. Suffice it to say, we had quite a wedding!

Rumpelstiltskin

Rumpelstiltskin. I heard that word somewhere. Sounds like a good word to me. I don't know what it means, but that never kept a good word out of circulation. I've used this word a number of times with surprising effects.

I tried it first on some of my fellow ducks. This was after my glorious adventure with the dog, and I had a reputation to cash in on. Three of my fellow ducks and I were out in the horse trough. We were doing some navigation drills, and the horses didn't seem to mind. Anyway, they were on the other side of the pasture.

The only way you can get up into the trough is to fly up and land on the edge. It's a big metal thing. Kind of hard on webbed feet. The edge is very narrow. Sharp as a meat cleaver. Well, not really. I have only a vague idea of what a meat cleaver is. It exists in the land beyond, and no one ever comes back to tell about it. Kind of like a holy book, which is full of ideas we can't prove.

I've heard about that too from the pigeons. Pigeons are commuter birds. They take short trips round about and leave a message. They leave messages all over the farm. But so do the rest of us. The master or his son shovel messages out of the henhouse sometimes. I don't know where they store them. I've heard they put them out in the fields, but that doesn't make sense. What does a field know?

Anyway, some of our pigeons have been to a place called a church. They get up in the bell tower and listen for rumors. Boy, do they hear them! There's no place like a bell tower for finding out all about the neighbors. That's before the service though. During the service, they worship a god who doesn't bother to show up. Now imagine that. I sure don't understand.

The pigeons say there's a book there too that no one can question because God wrote it. It even says God wrote it. But God never shows up to say why. If I wrote a book, I'd want to be there to get the credit. Well, he gets the credit anyway. I guess he knows that.

The point is . . . . The point is . . . . I have to admit there isn't any point. I don't know what I'm jabbering about. Quack, quack, quack all day long. That's all I ever do. It's all any of us ever do. But it sure is fun. That's how civilization progresses.

Getting back to my original line of thought. Getting back . . . . What was I thinking about? Let's see. Water, horses, metal, meat cleaver. Meat cleaver! No. Calm down. It's not that time yet. Oh yes, we were doing our navigation drills.

There are different ways of conducting these exercises. Very precise, of course. Very martial. We can go in a single column and sometimes do. That way you can cut like a knife through reeds and cattails. Of course, there aren't any reeds and cattails in a horse trough. On a small farm you have to improvise.

There's the flanking maneuver as well. That's when you send a duck or two out on either side. It increases the range of observation, prevents ambushes from snapping turtles, if they don't come from deep under, and reduces casualties during an artillery barrage. I've never experienced artillery, but I've heard about it from some of our wild cousins. Though it usually happens before they get into the water. Antiaircraft, I suppose.

Strange thing. I just realized I'm talking about maneuvers, and I haven't even gotten into the water yet. I have trouble telling a story. Kind of like turning around and around in a pond, looking for a succulent morsel underwater. I tell things from the outside, moving towards the center. It's a little confusing for some folks.

So my three friends are up in the trough. No problem. Up they go, a perfect landing on the edge, a wiggling of the tail, one deposit for the road, and, kerplash, in they go. They're circling around in there. I can just see their heads, and I can see there's no order to what they're doing. They need the old drill master.

Problem is, being a little older and more experienced, I'm a little heavier too. Gotta store all that wisdom somewhere. Can I make it? That's the question. So I beat my wings and create a considerable dust storm, but no liftoff. It's embarrassing. I give the wings a bit of a shake, wiggle my tail, make a deposit, and hit the accelerator. It's metal to the pedal this time.

Up I go in a whirlwind of dust, like an inverted tornado coming from the ground instead of the sky. Well, in all that dust I couldn't even see the edge of the trough. I went right over. Heck, I went over the whole thing and ended up on the other side. "Just a little aerial display," I said as I was passing over, not wanting to admit my mistake.

I could see them below me, their heads turned quizzically to one side, one eye looking up. They seemed a little dismayed. Lots of busy quacking by the time I hit the ground again. I couldn't catch the drift of it, but it didn't sound complimentary.

"Rumpelstiltskin!" I shouted and hit the air waves again. I was traveling faster than a radio signal. I wasn't going to make that mistake again. I roared off the ground like a Titan rocket, and then I hit the brakes in the air, right over the trough. You should've seen it. A brilliant maneuver. Came to a dead stop and plunged downward into the water. What a finish! Water rising like an inverted deluge. Water sloshing in the tank and spilling over. Ducks sloshing back and forth like the remains of a freshly sunk ship. One of them actually went over the side.

It took a few minutes, but our lost comrade finally returned to us in his usual graceful manner. First the side, then a delicate little skinny dip. So effeminate! But I didn't say anything.

Once we were all settled in the still sloshing tank, one of them asked, "What was that?"

"What was what?" I said, calmly putting my feathers back in order.

"Oh, nothing," he said, exchanging glances with the other two ducks.

But before we could get into maneuvers, we noticed a problem, a kind of storm brewing up out on the horizon. Two of the horses had seen the commotion and were heading back our way. Curiosity, I suppose, but oh those big teeth! Did you know you can probably fit an entire duck into the mouth of a horse? Even me, and that's going communal in one person.

I realize horses aren't carnivores. They don't eat meat. We do sometimes, but those are bugs, or maybe a snail or pollywog delicacy if there's a pond available. You can always tell a delicacy by its slippery texture. That's what makes it delicate. Hard to hold on to. Like a human eating uncooked eggs, raw fish, or caviar. It the easy slide that elevates the experience.

The problem was that to those horses we might look like leafhoppers on their lettuce. We weren't waiting to find out. When they got close enough, we were airborne, all of us at once, leaving silver trails of water behind us. This startled the horses, especially since I had to let out a little triumphant yell. I said, "Geronimo!" That's another version of rumpelstiltskin.

The horses scattered, we scattered, the water scattered, and the master came at a dead run.

Get out of there, you damned ducks," he shouted. He must've been thinking of the incident at the grain bin, and I hoped he didn't recognize me. "Fouling the horse water. Damn!"

You know, I was thinking about it after we got back into the barnyard. Is that why they call us fowl? And how about a foul ball? That's like a bird deposit too. Nobody seems to like them either.

Back in the barnyard, the first thing my erstwhile comrades said to me was, "What was that?"

"They were horses," I said.

"No, not that. That weird yell."

"Oh," I said a little sheepishly, quieting the volume of my quacks. "That."

"Yes, that. What was it?"

It was . . . . it was . . . . a rebel yell," I answered embarrassed.

"A rebel yell."

"Yes. A rebel yell."

The three of them stood there looking at me, shaking their beaks. "A rebel yell," they repeated to each other, wandering off. "He let out a rebel yell. What on earth for?"

Well, I knew what it was for. And I'm not the first misunderstood genius that ever lived. Someday they'll dig me up and transfer me to a mausoleum. You'll see.

These events greatly reduced the reputation I had earned with the dog. I was looked upon now as a bit of an eccentric. One of those fellas that carry a sign around saying, The world is coming to an end. But I knew the day would come when my true worth would be recognized.

All the same, I could hear both ducks and chickens saying in the days following, "He must've attacked the dog out of craziness, that's all. Sheer craziness. Eccentric old fellow." Even some of the pigeons were spreading this rumor about.

Well, the day of my vindication did finally come. But it wasn't the dog like before. It was the young master himself. The crazy one with the ax. It seems he got wind of my attack on his dog. The dog was acting afraid of ducks now, and not too sure about chickens either. That set the young master's teeth on edge. How could a boy be a man, when he had a cowardly dog?

So one day in the not too distant future he came out into the barnyard, walked right up to the stump, and picked up the ax. He had a wicked grin on his face—especially with some teeth missing—that made him look like a jack o' lantern. You know, one of those leering carved pumpkins, whose faces cave in when they dry out. Like a corpse left to dry out in the desert sun.

Okay, okay. I'm showing a little prejudice here. I never did like the kid. His father's bad enough, even if he does feed us. But the kid, well, you never know what he's going to do. Why didn't the master and his woman make a duck or a chicken instead of a kid? Ducks and chickens are good for all kinds of things. What's a kid good for, besides causing problems?

That's what he did too. He grabs the ax and starts running around the yard with it, threatening everything in sight. Even the pigeons, and they're such awful gossips, you'd think humans would like them. I think what he wanted to do was impress his dog. The thick-headed beast just sat there on its humble heavy haunches and cocked its head to one side. Its tail was wagging a bit, but not much. The dog couldn't make anything out either.

None of us could. This was sheer craziness. The boy going around in circles, swinging the ax, the dog sitting there, and ducks and chickens going every which way, running, flying, quacking, and squawking. Pandemonium.

Then suddenly I thought, What am I doing? Oh sure, the chickens are in a panic. They always are. But we're ducks. What are we doing? Acting like chickens, that's what. This has got to stop.

On the other hand, have you ever seen an ax whirling through the air at the end of a boy's arm? There never was a cobra more menacing, with its puffed up hood and all. You don't really want to stop for a chat in a situation like that. So I kept on running, staying out of reach as best I could, just like everyone else. We were of one accord: to have fled is better than to be dead.

But a thought did cross my mind in those panicked moments. What if one of us, me namely, was to steer him out of the barnyard? So I got up what was left of my winded courage, made a U-turn, and passed right in front of him, shouting, "Geronimo! Rumpelstiltskin!" and whatever I could think of at the top of my lungs.

That got his attention, let me tell you. He bore down on me like a cape buffalo, and me without a cape. I shot down and around the henhouse fast as I could go, him hot as dragon's breath on my neck. I barely cleared the henhouse, knocking some flight feathers loose when my wing hit the back corner of it. He slammed directly into the wall.

It was an unexpected piece of good fortune because he was out cold. Colder than dry ice in the palm of your hand. Actually, that's pretty hot, but you know what I mean. Wait a minute. What hand? Ducks have got no hands. It doesn't matter anyway.

The point is, all was peaceful again. The master and his woman came running out of the house to save their little boy and carried him back into the house like a bag of grain. The rest of us just stood around in the barnyard, raising our heads in innocent curiosity. We made a point of being quiet too. No sense stirring up another fuss.